In the **Beginner Reader** level, **Ste**
learned in previous steps, as chil

Special features:

Phonically decodable text builds reading confidence

Short sentences with simple language

"There is a tower near the pool," said Grandad. "We can go there and run up the stairs."

12

It began to rain.

"Shall we go back to the flat?" said Mark.

"All right," said Grandad.

13

Repetition of sounds in different words

Practice of words that cannot be sounded out

Summary page to reinforce learning

Story words

Can you match these words to the pictures?

hot-air balloon
classic cars
Fritha
tool kit
chairs

30

Tricky words

These tricky words are in the story you have just read. They cannot be sounded out. Can you memorize them and read them super fast?

are
were
out
what
be
was
said
have
some

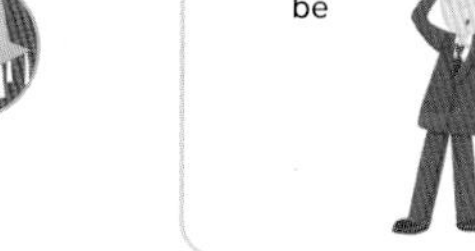

31

Ladybird

Educational Consultants: Geraldine Taylor and James Clements
Phonics and Book Banding Consultant: Kate Ruttle

LADYBIRD BOOKS

UK | USA | Canada | Ireland | Australia
India | New Zealand | South Africa

Ladybird Books is part of the Penguin Random House group of companies whose addresses can be found at global.penguinrandomhouse.com.

www.penguin.co.uk www.puffin.co.uk www.ladybird.co.uk

First published 2020
This edition published 2024
001

Written by Dr Christy Kirkpatrick

Illustrations by Hannah Wood

Printed in China

The authorized representative in the EEA is Penguin Random House Ireland, Morrison Chambers, 32 Nassau Street, Dublin D02 YH68

A CIP catalogue record for this book is available from the British Library

ISBN: 978-0-241-56438-7

All correspondence to:
Ladybird Books
Penguin Random House Children's
One Embassy Gardens, 8 Viaduct Gardens, London SW11 7BW

Visiting Grandad

Written by Dr Christy Kirkpatrick
Illustrated by Hannah Wood

Mark and Fritha went to Grandad's for the weekend.

Grandad was a big sports fan. Mark and Fritha saw Grandad jumping high.

"Let's get some fresh air," said Grandad.

Grandad took Mark and Fritha to the park. Grandad told them how to get the ball in the goal.

Next, they went to the swimming pool. Grandad was a quick swimmer.

The pool was a bit cool!

I'm not sure
I can do it!
It's freezing!

"There is a tower near the pool," said Grandad. "We can go there and run up the stairs."

It began to rain.

"Shall we go back to the flat?" said Mark.

"All right," said Grandad.

Grandad, Mark and Fritha had fish and chips for dinner. Then, they all had a rest.

Mark and Fritha saw Grandad.
He had fallen asleep!

Story words

Can you match these words to the pictures?

Grandad	tower
swimming pool	football
chips	Mark

Tricky words

These tricky words are in the story you have just read. They cannot be sounded out. Can you memorize them and read them super fast?

The Car Festival

Written by Dr Christy Kirkpatrick
Illustrated by Hannah Wood

Grandad, Mark and Fritha were off to a car festival.

They sat on some chairs on the bus.

Bang! The bus let out a sudden hiss and groan.

Grandad let out a sigh.

"I think we are stuck," he said.

Some classic cars were next to the bus.

A hot-air balloon set down near the bus.

"Is this the meeting point for the festival?" said the man.

Mark and Fritha had a turn in the balloon. They had a look at the classic cars.

By now, it was getting dark.

"The car festival will be shut now," said Grandad.

"We had a festival right near the bus!" said Fritha. "It was the best bus trip ever!"

Story words

Can you match these words to the pictures?

hot-air balloon

classic cars

Fritha

tool kit

chairs

How Music is Made

CW00847735

Contents

Elaine Morris

Music

Music is the sound made by **instruments**.
Different instruments make sounds
in different ways.
Some instruments are blown
and some are banged.
Some instruments are **plucked**
and others are shaken.

drum

guitar
recorder
tambourine

How Sounds are made

Do you know how the sound of music is made?
When an instrument vibrates, it makes sounds that travel through the air. We hear music when these sounds reach our ears.
Musicians use different ways to make an instrument **vibrate**.

Drum

A drum has a thin **skin** stretched tightly over it. This is called a drumhead. Sticks are used to beat the drumhead. Beating the drumhead makes it vibrate.

A drum is a **percussion instrument**.

Guitar

A guitar has strings made of plastic or metal. The strings are stretched tightly down the neck of the guitar so that they vibrate when they are plucked. Pressing on the strings on the neck of a guitar makes different notes.

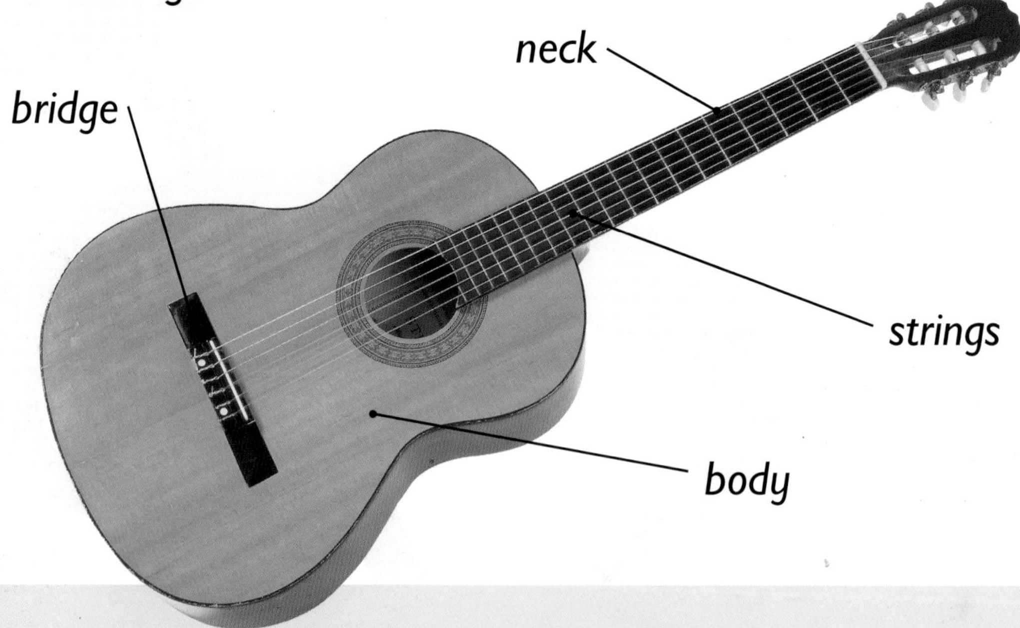

A guitar is a **string instrument**.

This guitar has six strings.

Recorder

At the top of a recorder is a mouthpiece. When someone blows down the mouthpiece, a small plug vibrates and makes a sound. Covering the holes in the recorder changes the **pitch** of the sound.

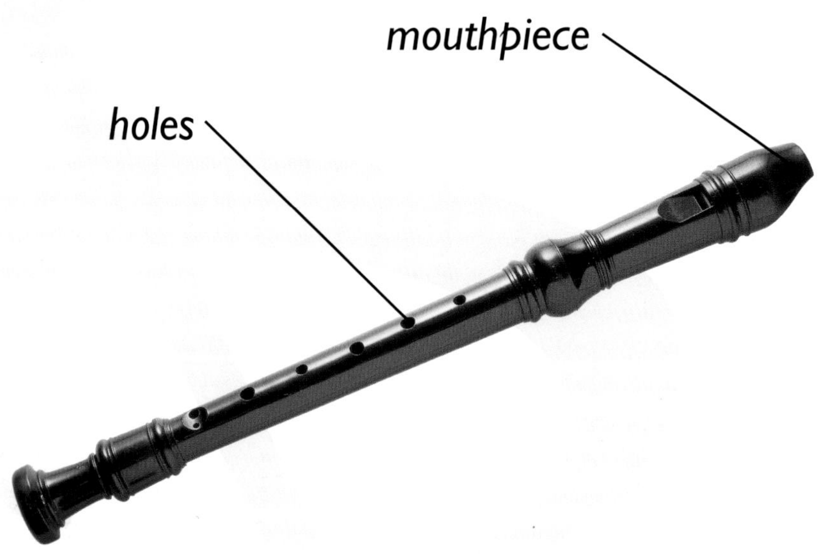

A recorder is a **wind instrument**.

Tambourine

A tambourine is a wooden ring with many small metal disks set into it. When a tambourine is shaken, the metal disks vibrate against each other to make a sound.

A tambourine is a percussion instrument.

More instruments

Are these wind, string or percussion instruments?

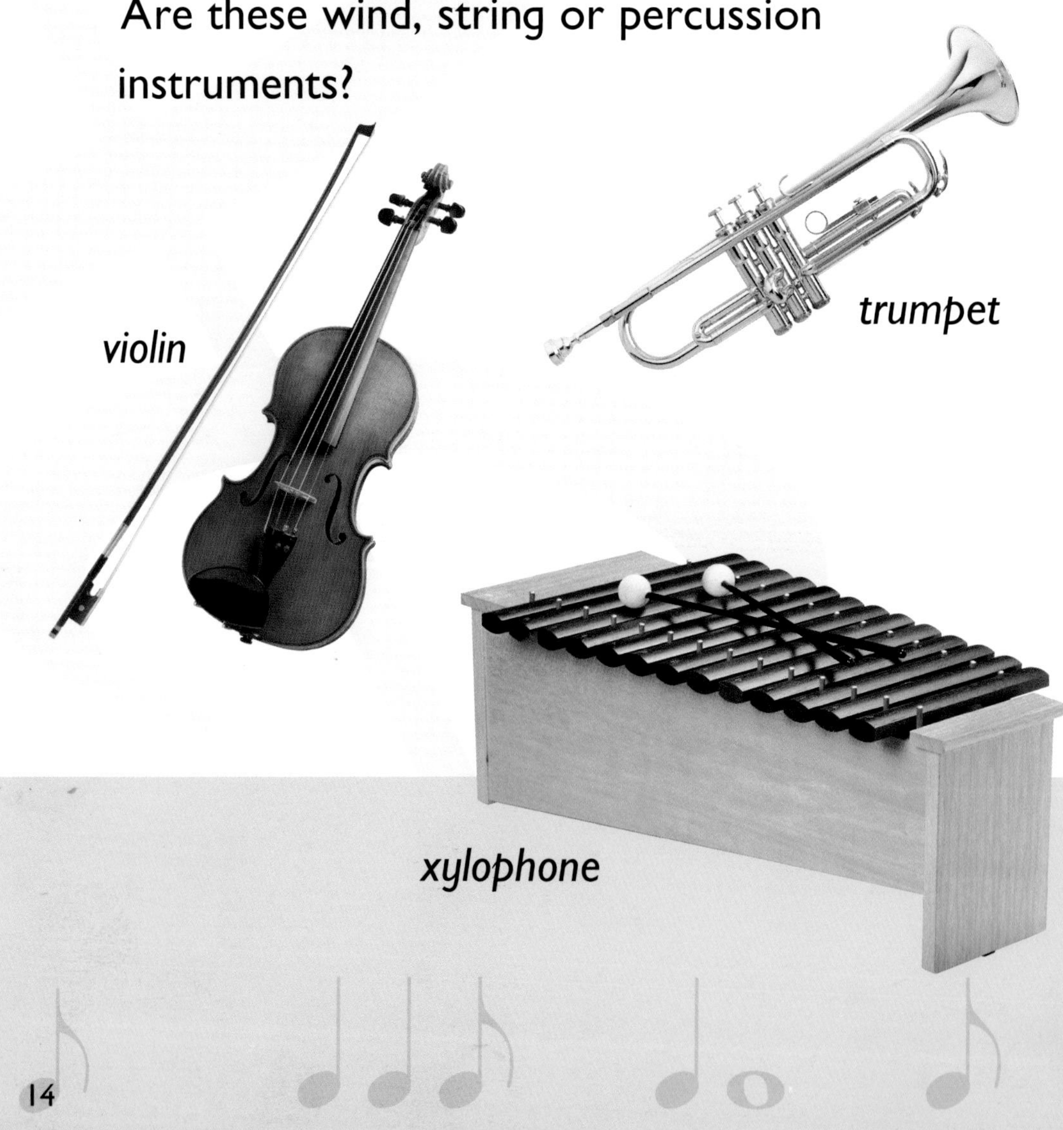

Glossary

instrument anything used to make music

musician anyone who makes music

percussion instrument an instrument played by beating it

pitch how high or low a sound is

pluck to pull with a finger and let go quickly

skin a thin cover stretched tightly over a drum

string instrument an instrument played by plucking or pressing its strings

vibrate moving forwards and backwards quickly

wind instrument an instrument played by blowing into its mouthpiece

Index